A CAPITAL OFFENSE

Joan Jedy

RCN Media Publishing

A Capital Offense by Joan Jedy © 2022 by RCN Media

First Edition: May 2022

RCN Media was founded in 2015 by Colton Nelson. It is a publishing company for adult, young adult and children's books. The RCN Media logo is © 2015 by Colton Nelson & RCN Media. If you require bulk orders of an issue with an RCN Media contact, feel free to contact them with the info below. Special discounts are available on quantity purchases by corporations, associations, and others. For details, contact the publisher at the email address below.

Artwork created and adapted by Colton Nelson.

Colton Nelson is the promoter for this book. For any comments or to contact the author, you can reach them through him (contact below), or you can contact RCN Media.

Contact:
www.rcn.media
(250) 206 0356
nelsoncolton16@gmail.com (subject: "A Capital Offense")

Also available as an eBook & Audiobook

1 3 5 7 9 0 2 4 6 8

ISBN: 978-1-989898-89-5

Also by Joan Jedy

Secrets of a Town Cursed
Banished to the Fifth Planet

Under the name Joan Donaldson-Yarmey

MYSTERIES
A Killer Match
Illegally Dead
The Only Shadow in the House
Whistler's Murder
Gold Fever

CANADIAN HISTORICAL
Romancing the Klondike
West to the Bay
West to Grande Portage

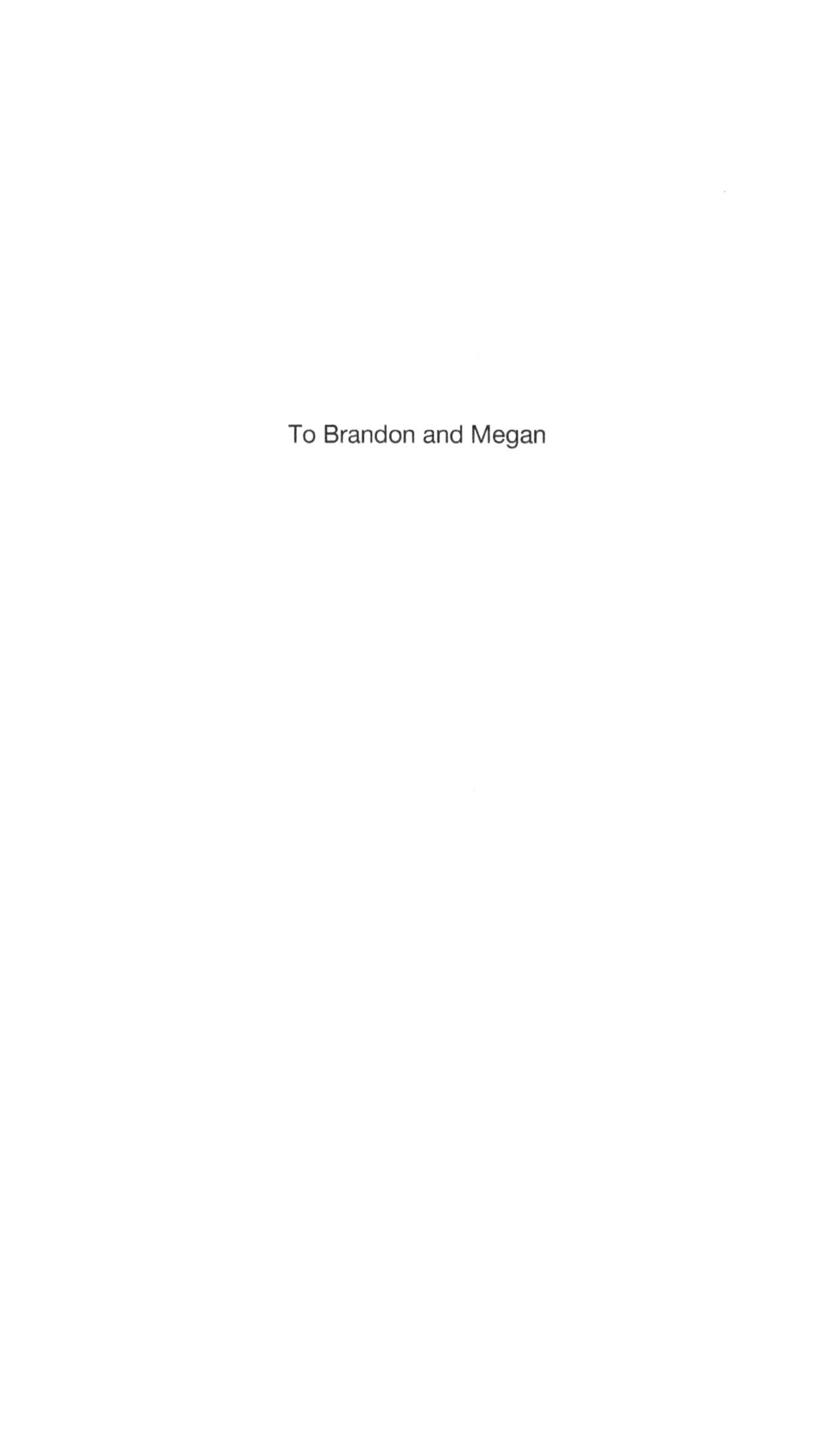

To Brandon and Megan

A NEW TWIST

I HESITATED OUTSIDE the door and took a deep breath. It was Wednesday evening and the first class of my seven-week short story writing course. I exhaled and walked into the room. There was a long table with seven chairs around it, three of which were filled. I smiled tentatively at the other aspiring writers as I sat down.

"My name is Paul," the only man at the table stated and looked expectantly at the rest of us.

"Lisa," I said.

"Frances, although everyone calls me Frankie."

"Marie."

"Doesn't look like there will be many in the class." Paul smiled.

"I've heard the instructor likes to keep the class small to give more attention to each student," Marie said.

"Have you written before?" Paul asked.

"I've tried a few short stories but can't get anything sold. So, I thought I'd take a writing course to find out what I am doing wrong. What about you?"

"I've bought many books on how to write plot and dialogue and how to create good characters, but I couldn't get any feedback from the books, so here I am."

"Any rejection slips?"

"I haven't had the guts to send anything to a magazine." He looked at Frankie. "Your turn."

"Basically, the same as yours. I've been getting frustrated because everything I write sounds so corny, so I thought I'd try for a professional opinion."

Before I could explain that I had done nothing in the way of writing previous to this course except wanting to write, the instructor entered the room and took the chair at the end of the table.

"My name is Stewart Manley, and I will be your teacher for the next six weeks," he began.

He paused and looked at us four students. "You have to be serious and determined to be a writer. And, as you can see, three would-be writers are not serious enough to even attend the first class. They will never be published."

Manley let that sink in, then continued. "You will have a short story completed by the end of this course, or you might as well give up trying to be a writer."

He stood and walked over to the blackboard. He wrote 'Plot', 'Theme', 'Characters', 'Setting', and 'Time Frame' in large letters. "These are the parts of a story. But before you can begin to write, you need an idea. This you may get from an incident you heard about on the radio or television or the internet, or from something that happened to you or someone you know. Once you have the idea, then you can start working on the characters, plot, theme, setting, and time frame."

Manley pointed to each word as he explained it. "You should have a main character and two supporting characters, one opposing the main character and the other on his or her side. The shorter the time frame in a story, the better the suspense. A fast-paced story spaced over a matter of hours gets the reader's blood rushing.

"The setting can be any place, a shop, a carnival, a craft show. The theme is the message you want to tell the reader and should be strong enough so the reader remembers it long after the story has faded."

Just then, a tall woman walked into the class. "Hi," she said as she took one of the empty seats. "I'm Cherise Hunter. Sorry, I'm late."

"Miss Hunter." Manley nodded. "Welcome."

***

I stared at the empty page of the scribbler. Tomorrow night was the second lesson of my writing course, and I needed an idea for a short story. I had to express it in three sentences, giving the plot, setting, the characters and their roles, and the theme.

But so far, none of my ideas had made much sense. I tried to remember something from the past week's news but failed. I thought of my friends, but none of them had much happening in their lives.

"Anyone can write a story," Manley had stated. "But not many can write a good story, and only a very few can write one worth publishing. If you work hard, by the end of the six weeks, you should have a publishable manuscript completed."

Since I couldn't even think of an idea for a short story, I couldn't see myself writing a publishable story in the next six weeks.

I stood and checked the potatoes. Almost done. The roast was cooked. Dirk would be home soon. Except for one niggling suspicion, my life was pretty mundane. Nothing to write about.

The phone rang. I scooped it up, expecting to hear my sister's voice. She usually called me on Tuesday nights.

"Honey, I won't be home until later," Dirk said.

"Again?" This was the third time in the past month.

"It's something I have to do."

"Okay," I sighed. "See you later."

I slowly hung up the phone. That niggling suspicion surfaced again, tenfold. For the five years of our marriage, Dirk had despised working overtime. He always said he would rather be home reading or watching television or working in his garden than using his time to make more money for the company. Why had he suddenly had a change of heart? Why was he so willing to remain in his office on nights when some of his favorite shows were on? The first night, I thought it might be an important account that he had to finish. The second time, I put it down to the argument we'd had that morning. This time, though, there could be only one explanation. My husband was having an affair.

I thought over what I had read about the telltale signs that showed a spouse might be seeing someone else. Dirk hadn't gone on a diet because he was in good shape. He hadn't bought different clothes, nor had he tried a new hair style or aftershave. The only thing he had done was buy a shaver to keep at work. At the time, he claimed he liked to be clean shaven when he met with clients. Now I knew the real truth. He didn't want to scratch her with his five o'clock shadow.

I shut the heat off under the potatoes and took the roast out of the oven. I paced the room, wondering what I should do, what I *could* do. I began to speculate about who she might be. Was she a coworker? Was she someone he had met on one of his infrequent visits to the bar with some of the guys from work? Was she someone he'd corresponded with on the internet? There were so many ways he could have met her.

To calm myself, and to take my mind off my suspicions, I picked up my scribbler and tried to concentrate on a story idea. What if I wrote about my husband's supposed affair? Would it make a good story? I could describe everything I did to find out who Dirk was seeing and use that as the plot. The setting would be wherever I discovered him to be. The theme: don't screw around on your spouse. The more I thought about it, the more I liked it.

Before I went that far, I figured I should check to make sure he wasn't at work. I dialed his number. No answer. Maybe he had just gone to the washroom. I dialed again. It went to his voicemail. I tried his cell phone. It was shut off. If he was working, he really didn't want to be disturbed; if he was with another woman, the same was true.

So, write the story I would. And, maybe as I wrote, I might get ideas on how to catch Dirk and his girlfriend together. I picked up my pen and wrote three sentences: *Maude suspects her husband is having an affair. She follows him until she sees him with his girlfriend. Will she confront him and maybe forgive, or will she kill him?*

When Dirk arrived home later, I feigned sleep. I could feel him stand over me. Did he want to tell me about it? Was he going to confess his infidelity? I prayed he wouldn't try to wake me. I hadn't had time to absorb the concept of his affair, the ramifications it would have on our marriage, and the thought that he might want a divorce. When he finally went to his side of the bed, I breathed a silent *thank you.*

The next morning, he smiled at me across the table. "Did you get an idea for your short story?"

I had told him about my first lesson, and he'd tried to help me with my idea, even reading some headlines from the newspaper.

"Yes," I answered.

"Good. Do you want to tell me about it?"

I shook my head. "I'd prefer to wait until it is written."

"I'm glad you're finally taking this writing course," he said, spreading jam on his toast. "I've come to believe that everyone should try something they've really wanted to do, that life is too short to put it off."

Was this his way of bringing up his affair? Was he trying to explain why he was seeing someone else? Was that what he wanted to tell me last night when he came home? I nodded, not knowing what to say.

He finished his toast and kissed me on the cheek. "I'll be home on time tonight."

I got my scribbler and wrote down our breakfast conversation.

We had just opened our books to our story ideas when Cherise Hunter walked in.

"Hi." She grinned. Last week she'd explained how she worked from seven at night to two in the morning every night except Wednesdays, when she worked days until six thirty. "I'm sorry," she'd said. "But I will always be a little late."

Her height sunk in again as she took the seat beside me, making me feel small and inadequate, just as I sometimes felt beside Dirk's six feet. I wasn't sure if it was because of size— I myself am five foot, four inches— or if it was because of her outgoing, friendly manner. People like that tended to overwhelm me.

"That's pretty common story material, Lisa," Manley said when I'd read my idea. "Unless it is based on truth and can bring in a new angle, I would suggest you find a different idea."

I had nothing else. "I'll stick with this one."

He went to the front of the room. "A short story is usually divided into four sections, with part one establishing the problem. The maneuvers the main character goes through to solve this problem constitute the plot. So, he or she must make wrong decisions before reaching the right one, or the story will end very quickly. The crisis is brought on by all the incorrect decisions, and the climax is reached when the problem is solved."

Manley sat behind his desk. "Now you can begin your short story. You have to set the problem, establish the characters, and describe the setting. I'll be here if you need any help."

I began writing: *Maude checked the potatoes. Almost done. And the roast was cooked. Dan would be home soon. Except for one niggling suspicion, her life was pretty mundane.*

The phone rang. She scooped it up, expecting to hear her sister's voice. She usually called Maude on Tuesday nights.

"Honey, I won't be home until later," Dan said.

"Again?"

When Dirk called Tuesday night to say he would be late, I was ready. I jumped in my car and raced over to the firm where he worked, hoping to get there before he left. I was in luck. I saw him pull out of the parking lot a block ahead of me, and I followed him. He headed downtown and turned into the Wilk's Hotel parking lot. The Wilk's was home to a strip club, plus a variety show on Tuesday and Thursday evenings featuring various local bands, a chorus line of tall, long-legged dancers, and some second-rate comedians.

Dirk entered through a side door, and I watched for a woman I might know to go in or for Dirk and a woman to come out. I cried as I sat and waited. Dirk left the building at ten-thirty looking the same as when he entered. No one was with him. I drove home like a maniac to get there ahead of him.

The next day my mood shifted from anxiety, to anger, to fear, to sadness, to confusion. I went over what I had believed to be our five good years together. Apparently, Dirk hadn't felt the same way about them. Unbidden tears fell. Was this the end of our marriage?

I managed to write about Maude suspecting her husband's affair, following him to the hotel (I disguised the name) and then trying to decide how to handle the situation. I made it to the third class that evening. Each student stood and read his or her work, and the rest of us made comments before Manley gave his opinion. I was impressed with the problems and settings of the others and began to doubt my choice.

When it was my turn, I stood and shyly read. At the end, Paul asked why it is always the husband who is the bad guy and has the affair. "I know lots of women who fool around on their husbands."

Somehow, I got through the next few days, and it was Tuesday again when Dirk phoned to say he was working late. This time he also mentioned that he would be late every Tuesday evening from now on. Was that the only night she was free to see him? I drove straight to the hotel. I thought about going inside and hiding somewhere, maybe behind a pillar in the lobby, but I was afraid he might see me.

Dirk pulled into the parking lot and again entered by the side door. Why didn't he go through the front doors? Was he afraid someone might see him, someone who would tell me?

The tears began again, but this time when they were over, my anger surfaced. What the hell did he think he was doing? What gave him the right to take on a girlfriend without even telling me what was wrong with our marriage? And what was that woman doing, seeing a married man? I felt like going in and finding Dirk and demanding answers to my questions, but then I realized I wasn't sure if I was ready for those answers.

I wondered what his girlfriend did in the hotel. Was she a singer or a comedienne or in the tall chorus line? Was she a stripper, and did he put money in her G-string when she danced in front of him? Did they rent a room and have sex all evening before going their separate ways? Did she live there?

"I work in a hotel," Cherise said the next evening, after I had read my week's writing. "Very few people actually live there on a long-term basis."

"You can't have a woman she recognizes walk in because that would eliminate the build-up of who she is," Manley said. "But you can't have Maude sitting out in her car night after night either. You must have her take some action in the next section."

I drove to the hotel early Tuesday evening, determined to go in. "Your marriage is at stake here," I said aloud. "And besides, Maude has to do something by tomorrow night."

I climbed out of the car and darted across the road into the hotel lobby. I looked around for a place to hide but didn't see any of the large, bushy plants that were in every hotel lobby in the movies. I hurried through the open door into the lounge and found a seat where I could watch the side door.

When the waitress came to take my order, I asked for a Shirley Temple. I would need my wits about me if I was going to follow Dirk without him seeing me. At precisely six-thirty, Dirk came through the door. I suddenly began to sweat. What if he entered the lounge? He would immediately see me. I breathed a sigh of relief as he headed in a different direction.

When he was out of sight, I rushed to the doorway and saw him walk down a hallway. He stopped at a door, knocked, and when it opened, entered. I wanted to go read the number on the door but reasoned that he might come out again. I quickly weighed my options and went to a table at the far end of the lounge near the washrooms. If they came in, I would have time to duck into the ladies and even stay there all night if I had to. Dirk certainly wouldn't come in and find me.

A country and western band with a young female singer came on stage. She had a lovely voice and sang a few songs. Dirk and his girlfriend hadn't shown up by the time they were finished, so I decided it was time to check the room number. By now they were probably sipping wine and thinking about the rest of the evening.

As much as I wanted to sneak down the hallway on my tiptoes, I forced myself to walk normally. I strolled past the door and looked at the number out of the corner of my eye. 111.

I stopped at the end of the corridor. To my left was an exit, to my right another hallway. I should have left by the exit, but I wanted so badly to burst into 111 and catch them together. I turned and went back to the door, where I hesitated. Right then, Dirk's affair was just an assumption. To knock and have them open the door would make it a reality. I headed back to the lobby.

The second show was the chorus line, but I really didn't want to watch a group of tall, slender women kick their heels above their heads and do all sorts of complex dance steps on the stage. I returned to my car, my spirits low. Then I began to shake, and tears rolled down my cheeks. I loved Dirk, and now he was fooling around on me. What was I going to do? Should I pretend I knew nothing and hope it would soon end, or should I confront him with what I knew and demand that he quit seeing her?

"Quit seeing who?" Frankie asked when I had presented my week's work. "Maude hasn't actually seen him with another woman."

"But there is so much evidence," I said. "He says he's working late when he isn't. He goes to the hotel and into a room. What is she supposed to think?"

"Why doesn't Maude find out who rents that room?" Paul asked.

I had thought about it but hadn't come up with a good reason for requesting that information. "How?" I asked hopefully.

"It's your story," Manley said. "You decide how to do it."

To write the next part of my story, I entered the hotel the following Tuesday morning and went straight to the reception desk before I could chicken out.

"Excuse me," I said to the woman. "I would like a room on the ground floor, and I'd like it to be number 111 because 1 is my lucky number." It was the best I could come up with.

The woman looked at me as if I was crazy. "That room is already taken. We could give you 112."

"That won't do." I tried to keep my voice steady. "Who is renting that room?"

"We don't give out that information."

My knees shook. "I just need her name."

"I think you'd better leave before I call security," the woman said coldly.

I left, and it took me a few minutes to calm down before I drove away. I went to a store and purchased a cheap black wig to cover my light brown hair. I donned the wig that night and put on more than my usual makeup. When I saw my face in the mirror with its shadowed eyes, rouged cheeks, and bright red lips, I was sure Dirk wouldn't recognize me. I decided to arrive later for the second show. His girlfriend must be in the chorus line.

As I quickly crossed the lobby to the lounge door, a tall woman emerged from room 111. I stopped dead in my tracks, my mouth open. That was Dirk's girlfriend, my competition, the woman who had caused me so many sleepless nights and red eyes. My mind digested the abundance of shoulder-length blonde hair and the full-length pink gown with thigh-high slits, long sleeves, and a ruffled neckline. My insides crumbled as I suddenly understood Dirk's affair. He liked tall women, women who were flashy and lively, not short, mousy women like me.

The woman went down the hall and around the corner. I was too far away to make out her face, but there was something familiar about her. Maybe it was her walk, the way she held her shoulders, or her hair. I couldn't tell what it was, but I knew I'd seen her before.

I closed my mouth and forced myself to enter the lounge. I ordered another Shirley Temple and sat at the same table by the washrooms. I kept my eyes on the door waiting for Dirk to come in to watch the show. The eight tall women, dressed in identical pink gowns, twirled across the stage, swinging their arms and shaking their booties at the audience, which drew cheers from the male audience members. I had finally confirmed what Dirk's girlfriend did in the hotel.

But where was Dirk? Why wasn't he watching her show? Had he seen it so often that he was bored and just waited for her in the room? I sadly sipped my drink and tried not to visualize Dirk and one of these women in bed, partaking in the raw, steamy sex that only happened in romance books. I was brought out of my reverie by the sound of applause as the dancers finished their number and started another high-kicking routine.

The sixth class had us finishing the crisis and working towards the climax.

"You have to make sure the ending is a grabber, something different from any other story of this type," Manley said again to me. "You can't just have Maude kill her husband or his girlfriend or both."

I nodded. I knew that, but since I didn't know how my story was going to end, I didn't know how Maude's would either.

I sat for the last time watching the hotel. I had made up my mind to walk down that hallway and knock on the door fifteen minutes after Dirk entered the hotel. It was time to end the uncertainty and deal with the truth.

I strode past the desk and along the hall to room 111, my hand clenched in a fist. Before I could talk myself out of it, I pounded on the door. I stepped back, my heart fluttering. I didn't care who answered, Dirk or his girlfriend. I'd rehearsed a speech for each of them.

But when the door opened, all I could do was stare.

"Lisa? What...what are you doing here?"

I shook my head slowly. "I... I thought you were having an affair."

"An affair?" he asked, confused. "Why would you think that?"

"The lies about working late, the nights spent here."

"But I'm working here."

"I see that." I looked at his long pink dress and partial makeup.

Dirk reddened. "I tried to tell you, but I didn't think you would understand."

"And I don't."

"It's something I found I like to do."

"And how did you find that out?"

"By coming with a buddy from work who's been dancing here for six months."

"You mean, there are other men in that show?" I thought about the strutting and high kicks. Not once had I suspected any of them to be men.

"They're all men."

"All of them?"

"All of them."

We were quiet for a moment.

"And now I suppose you're thinking that it would have been better if I'd been having an affair."

Actually, I was thinking Manley would have to admit this was certainly a new twist on the old story.

DOUBLE CROSS

HARRY WAS HUNCHED forward in his wheelchair. He ignored the person beside him as he stared out the tall window overlooking the wide expanse of lawn. He was angry, so very angry. But there was nothing he could do about the cause of that anger. He'd always felt that each year of his life had gone by fast, that he hadn't accomplished all the things he'd wanted to do. But it was the last three years that he was truly angry about. And it was those years that his mind dwelled on now.

Four years ago, Harry was peering around the corner of a building and scouring a dark alley. He knew they were in there waiting for him, the men who wanted to take over his share of the city's drug trade. He could see the faint light at the other end of the alley and the hulks of the garbage dumpsters. The men could be hiding behind any of them or in doorways.

Harry motioned for his four associates to enter ahead of him. They were dressed in black and quickly blended into the murkiness as they hugged the walls. He waited for the first burst of gunfire, and it came shortly. Three men jumped up from behind a dumpster and started shooting. His three henchmen stationed at the other end stepped into the light and took them out quickly. Two more leaped out of doorways. One of his men went down. A few more volleys and it was over.

Whoever had been behind the takeover attempt hadn't been very smart or organized. For one thing, the setup had been so obvious: some guy wanting to buy an unusually large amount of meth and wanting to meet in an alley at night. Harry could have ignored it or just sent his men to take care of it, but he'd decided to make an example of them, show others that he was still on top of his game. That he wasn't a fool.

Two of Harry's men grabbed their fallen associate, and they all jumped into the waiting cars, squealing away from the alley. Harry didn't care who the dead men were or who they worked for. It didn't really matter. He'd learned long ago that he couldn't let his guard down for one minute, not even with men he trusted.

Harry leaned his head against the backrest. He was fifty-five years old and tired of worrying about being shot by a business rival. He was tired of having to watch his back all the time, and he didn't want to deal with traitors within his own organization anymore. The other car turned off onto a side street where their doctor ran his private practice. Either the injured man would be treated and kept until better or declared dead and buried before dawn.

Back at his home, Harry waved to the men who guarded his mansion. He went upstairs to his bedroom, but instead of changing into pajamas and going to bed, he picked up the scrap of paper he'd been given a few days ago.

In his line of work, there was always someone who had a connection to someone who knew someone who had heard of someone. Nothing was ever a true secret. It was just a matter of getting the word to the right person.

There had been whispers about a disgraced doctor/researcher who had set up a cloning and face-restructuring enterprise. Two weeks ago, Harry had discreetly put word out on the street, offering ten thousand dollars to whoever could give him a name.

He'd had one taker and was supposed to meet him in an hour. Harry opened his safe and took out the envelope with the money in it. He slipped it in the front of his waistband and touched his gun flat against his back. He might need it.

Because he didn't want anyone to know his plans, he had to sneak out alone. When he first moved into the house, he'd had the master bedroom renovated to include a secret room. A passageway led from there to his basement and then connected to the house next door. No one knew that house was in his long-dead sister's name. He went to the garage and started the car he kept there. He had long ago taken out the interior light bulbs and used the override button to disable the automatic headlight system to control when the headlights shone. Harry pressed the switch to raise the garage door and drove quietly away.

Instead of parking in front of the fitness store at the outlet mall, he drove around the darker areas looking for other vehicles. There were none. The cleaning staff must have finished up already. He parked four stores away and shut off the car. Could this be another trick, another attempt on his life? Should he have brought some backup? He stared around. Nothing moved, there were no slinking shadows, no sudden bright light shone in his face.

Harry patted his gun again, then climbed out of his car and walked to the front of the store. Rather than going around to the back as instructed, he leaned against the window so he could see in all directions. If the person wanted his money, they had to come to him in the open.

"Harry?"

Harry looked over to see a head peeking around the corner of the building. "Yes."

The man looked around and then slunk over. "Joey."

Harry nodded.

"Got the money?"

"Got the info?"

"Yes." Joey glanced left and right. "But I was warned against going to the cloning company."

"Warned? Why?"

"There is something wrong with their clones, but no one has an idea what it is."

"Then how do they know?"

"Because there aren't any satisfied customers."

"What about dissatisfied customers?"

"There aren't any of them either."

"Then what seems to be the problem?" Harry asked in exasperation. He wanted the name, not a lecture.

"There are no customers to talk to."

"Well, that's probably because it is against the law." Enough talk. "Who is this organization?"

"Speigler Corporation."

"Speigler? Weren't they just in the news about something?"

"Yeah, they just completed another senior citizen's facility. It's the second one in three years."

"So, how do I get in touch with the cloning section?" He wasn't sure if that was the name to use.

"There is no cloning section."

"Well, who do I contact?"

"I've heard a guy named Al. You have to say you want to see him about making a $102,000 donation to the corporation's research department."

"Why is that?"

"Because that is what a clone costs, and it has to be in cash. They want $50,000 up front."

"Thanks, Joey. Here's the money I owe you." He handed over the envelope.

While Joey was counting the money, Harry pulled out his gun and shot him. He didn't need word getting out about what he was doing. He picked up the money and left.

The next morning, Harry walked into the Speigler Corporation building and asked for Al.

"What do you want to see him about?" the receptionist asked.

"I want to make a $102,000 donation to the research department."

"May I have your name?"

"Harry Zimmerman."

"Just a minute, sir."

She lifted the receiver on the phone and pressed a number. “There’s a man here who wants to make a donation.” She listened a moment, then hung up. “Someone will be here shortly. Have a seat while you wait.”

Harry sunk down in one of the overstuffed leather chairs in the reception area. He’d just gotten settled when a woman walked up to him. She held out her hand.

“Hi, I’m Sue,” she said pleasantly. “I’ll take you to see Al.”

She led him to an elevator. There were no buttons for the floors above. They descended past B1, B2, B3, and at B4, the elevator stopped. When the doors opened, an older man with wispy gray hair and glasses was waiting for them.

“Harry Zimmerman?”

“Yes.”

“I’m Al.” He beckoned Harry out of the elevator. The doors closed immediately behind him.

“I understand you wish to make a donation.” Al led Harry down a dimly lit hall to a small office. He sat down behind a desk and offered Harry a chair. “Just so you know up front, we make no guarantees on our products.”

“That’s a lot of money for no guarantee.”

“The choice is yours.”

Since there seemed to be no room for negotiation, Harry asked, “How long will it take to clone me?”

“Most clones take a year. If you want one with more of your memory, it will take longer.”

“A year? Isn’t that a long time?”

“That’s actually fast compared to our first ones. They begin as an embryo from your DNA, then we grow them through the stages of your life up to the age you are now. That is a lot of forced feeding of growth serum and memory intensifier.”

“How much will it know about my life?”

“It will know everything the DNA tells it. However, the memory may not be as quick as in the ones that go through the slower process."

"How much will he know about being a clone?"

"In his mind, you will be the clone."

Good. "If he happens to die, will it affect me?"

"So far, none of our clones have died, so we don't know."

"How long do they live?"

"Our oldest is six years."

"Are there any problems I should know about beforehand?"

"Like any other company, we are always working on ways to improve our product. We won't know if some of the past problems have been solved until the new clone has been put to use."

The answer sounded evasive to Harry but no different from what any other company would give. And Harry needed a clone badly, for work and for protection.

"What about secrecy?"

"Who are we going to tell? What we are doing is illegal."

"I'll take one," Harry said.

Al nodded. "That will be a $50,000 down payment, and the balance is due on delivery. I'm sure you were told cash."

Harry pulled the bulky envelope from his suit pocket. He waited while Al counted the five hundred $100 bills.

"Okay." Al returned the pile to the envelope. "There are some papers I need signed."

"No one said anything about signing papers," Harry grumbled. He didn't like the idea of his signature being on record anywhere."

"It's just to make sure we will be compensated if anything happens to you."

"So, if I die before the clone is complete, you still get your money from my estate?"

"Something like that."

Harry shrugged. "I'll be dead, so I guess it won't matter to me where my money goes. What happens to the clone if I die?"

"We look after him."

"At my expense, I imagine."

Al smiled as he brought out a sheaf of stapled papers from a desk drawer and handed it to Harry. Harry started to read the first page and gave up. It was all legal speak and gobbledygook to him. He looked at Al. "You know I will kill you if you try to screw me."

Al nodded. "Just initial each page so that I can't slip in anything extra."

Harry grinned and dropped the papers on Al's desk. He took a pen from his shirt pocket and quickly flipped through the pages, initialing each one. On the last page, he signed on the dotted line. He pushed them towards Al.

"Come with me, and we will get the DNA sample."

A year later to the day, Harry carefully checked out his clone. He opened its eyelids to make sure its eyes were the same shade of blue as his. He held his hands to its hands; they were the same size. So were the feet. He took a tape and measured its waist, its leg and arm length, and its hat size. He'd brought some hair from his last trim and held it to its head. The colour matched exactly. Al gave him a mirror, so he could see both their faces at once.

"Remarkable," Harry said, impressed.

"Now, because the clone contains your DNA, his appearance and actions will be just like yours. He will have your thought process, but like I said a year ago, his memory won't be quite the same."

"You said that he will think of me as the clone."

"Yes." Al nodded.

"Is that going to be a problem?"

"Other than the fact that he will want to give the orders, I don't think so."

"Good. Now how does he come to life?"

"He's already alive," Al said. "He's been given a sedative that will wear off while we go to my office and do the final paperwork."

When they returned, the clone was fully awake and dressed in the clothes Harry had brought. It gave Harry a jolt to see himself standing there. The new Harry seemed surprised, also.

"Hello," Harry said cautiously.

"Hello," Harry Two said, in the exact same voice.

"What is your name?"

"Harry Zimmerman."

"Where do you live?"

"1828 Broadmoor Street." The tone and inflection were the same as Harry's.

"This is so perfect." Harry grinned.

Harry Two grinned back, then turned to Al. "He likes to ask questions, doesn't he?"

Harry had given the household staff the day off, so he would have time to give his clone a tour of the house. He wanted to see how much Harry Two already knew and was pleasantly impressed when Harry Two acted as if he'd lived there as long as Harry himself. Harry had already transferred his things into the secret room, and Harry Two took over the master bedroom.

It quickly became apparent that Harry Two was assuming control. When staff returned the next day, he gave them orders just as Harry would have done.

Right from the start, Harry noticed a difference. He was able to keep a better eye on the books and watch for skimming; he was able to conduct more private meetings; and he could relax knowing that the business was in good hands. His hands. He even took a holiday. None of his bodyguards knew of the change. When they were off with Harry Two, Harry could move around as he pleased.

And he found he liked cheese. He hadn't before, but when Harry Two began eating it, Harry felt the same urge. He wondered if, somewhere back in his own memory, he'd liked cheese but had forgotten about it until Harry

Two's memory had brought it to the surface.

After the first year, he noticed his hair, which had been gray at the temples, became liberally sprinkled with gray, as did Harry Two's. Both their faces had a few more wrinkles, and Harry felt more aches and pains than before. He was surprised. He'd thought that with the stress of the job relieved, he would look and feel more youthful. He went to the doctor for a complete check-up, and nothing was wrong.

"You're just getting old," the doctor told him.

During the second year, Harry's joints began to bother him, and he had a hard time getting up in the morning. Liver spots appeared on his hands, and his hair turned totally white. When he looked at Harry Two, he recognized his father's face, his father at 75. This scared him.

"You're just aging like everyone else," the doctor said.

But Harry didn't believe that. He was only fifty-eight. He went to the Speigler Corporation to find out why this was happening.

The receptionist took Harry down to B4.

Al listened patiently to Harry's complaints.

"Yes, we've had other people say the same thing," Al said. "And we think we finally know what the problem is."

"What is it?" Harry demanded. "And how are you going to fix it?"

"Well, as you know, Dolly the sheep was the first cloned animal," Al said quietly. "She didn't live very long, dying at an early age for a sheep. After much study, the geneticists believe that she aged faster than a normal sheep. And that has been true of any animal clones since then."

Fear gripped Harry. "What does that have to do with me aging?"

"Well, we've had the same problem with our human clones. It seems that the DNA in your clone is controlling the DNA in your body, and you are aging as fast as your clone."

Harry's fear turned to anger. "Why, if you knew of this, did you sell me my clone?" he yelled.

"Well, we have to raise money for our research," Al said, pushing a button on his desk. "It's not as if the government is offering us assistance."

"So, you knew this would happen to me when I came to you." Harry wanted to punch Al, hard.

"Not exactly. We'd changed some of our procedures and were hoping they would work. Apparently, they didn't."

Harry wished he'd brought a gun with him. Then he had a thought. "What happens if I kill him? Will the aging slow down again?"

"It has worked for other originals, but it doesn't work for the clones who think they are the originals."

Just then the door opened, and a large man stood in the doorway. "Frank will see you out," Al said.

During the next year, Harry tried to kill his clone, but Harry Two was on his guard. Harry himself had begun to keep a vigilant watch. There'd been a few close calls with his car that he suspected Harry Two was behind. Hiring someone to kill Harry Two was out of the question. What if they killed the wrong man?

Al began visiting, citing a desire to keep track of the changes that were taking place in both Harry and his clone. He took pictures of them as their bodies aged at a rapid rate.

Eventually, neither Harry nor his clone could go out in public anymore. Harry didn't want his rivals to see him in his frail state. When he could no longer climb the stairs, he fired his staff and bodyguards and hired nurses, telling them he and Harry Two were twins. He took over the downstairs guest bedroom, and Harry Two was relegated to the library, where a single bed was set up.

Harry lost power over his men, and it wasn't long before they stepped in and began making deals with his drug connections. In a matter of three years, Harry was transformed from a fierce, virile force in the drug business to a frail old man who couldn't look after himself.

One day, Al arrived with two ambulances. "Time to move you to a seniors' home."

"What?" Harry sputtered. He hated that his voice sounded so creaky. "You can't do that. You have no legal right."

"According to your signature, I have the right to enact Power of Attorney when I deem it necessary."

"I didn't sign any such thing."

Al produced a sheaf of papers from his briefcase. "Remember these?"

"I'll tell the court I didn't know what I was signing."

"Too late. The courts have already approved my application. All it took was this paper and the pictures I have been taking to show your decline."

Once Harry and Harry Two were settled at one of the Speigler Corporation owned seniors' homes, Al sold Harry's mansion and put the money into a fund for genetics and geriatric research.

Two nursing attendants approached the two wheelchairs and unlocked their brakes. "It's time to put you to bed, Misters Zimmerman," one attendant said pleasantly.

Harry tried to straighten his back but couldn't. His hands were like claws as he gripped the afghan that covered his spindly legs. He glanced over at his clone, who looked back at him, the mirror image of an old man.

On the way down the hall they passed other rooms, all with elderly twins in them. There were no rooms for single residents in the building.

AFRAID OF HEIGHTS

IT'S FUNNY HOW *many people are so trusting. Some walk with their heads down, eyes glued to their cell phones, minds oblivious to the people around them. They have no idea that someone may be watching them. Others have earbuds in their ears, listening to music as they stroll along. They have no idea that someone may be sneaking up behind them. And it is amazing how many people are so naive around heights. They stand on balconies twenty stories up, believing they are safe. They walk along the edges of cliffs, believing that the ground won't fall out from under them. They climb towers believing that they will get back down safely. They don't question the motives of the person next to them. It doesn't enter their minds that their lives could be in that person's hands.*

For instance, take the couple who were leaning on the railing of the deck overlooking a wide valley with a river winding through it. They were discussing whether they wanted to climb the 100-foot-high Temagami Fire Tower that stood behind them. The young woman was all eager, but the young man was hesitant. Were they in love? Had they both wanted to come here or only one of them? What if that one had thoughts about pushing the other off the top of the tower?

I had been on a road trip through Ontario for a week when I saw the road sign advertising the Temagami Fire Tower as a tourist attraction with wonderful views. It was early evening when I pulled into the parking lot. I walked to the tower to see the view from the security of the centre of the deck.

Then, after seeing them, I decided to wait for the young couple to make up their minds about climbing the tower.

***

I AM AFRAID OF heights. At least I think it is of heights. Maybe it isn't so much that as it is a fear of falling from that height. Whichever it is, I have had that fear since I was eight years old and on a camping trip in the mountains with my family. The first morning, my parents decided that they, my brother Barry, and I should hike up a trail to a picnic area where we could eat lunch and look out over a large valley. We started out with my mother in the lead and my brother behind her. I was third and my father last. At first, the ground was basically flat, but soon the trail became steep with a drop-off on our right. We were about a half hour into the hike when Barry, who is three years older and a foot taller, started teasing me about how out of shape I was.

"You know you're slowing down our hike," he said the third time he and my parents had to stop and wait for me to have a drink of water. "And don't think you're fooling anyone by saying you're thirsty. We all know you're stopping to catch your breath."

"Am not," I protested, trying to control my breathing. I will admit I was a little overweight for my height, and since school had let out for the summer, doing any form of exercise had not been part of my day.

"Are too." Barry stuck his tongue out at me.

"That's enough," my mother said quietly.

I put the bottle of water into the holder on my day-hiker waist pack and adjusted it on my hips. We continued our trek.

It wasn't long before Barry pulled out one of his earbuds and looked over his shoulder. "Geez, you're panting like dog. You're making so much noise I can't hear my music."

By this time, I was getting frustrated and angry. I didn't know why my parents had thought this hike was a good idea for me. They were active people, bicycling and jogging in the summer and cross-country skiing in the winter. Barry played hockey in the winter and soccer in the summer. Me, I liked to lay on my bed and read or surf the internet. All seasons.

I reached out and gave Barry a shove to shut him up. He tripped and fell forward.

My father grabbed me from behind and thrust my upper body out over the drop-off. I screamed, my arms flailing at empty air. Stone-cold terror welled up in me.

"Do you see how far down that is?" Dad demanded. I barely heard him over the buzzing in my ears. "That's how far Barry would have fallen if you had pushed him harder." The rocks below floated through the haze that partly obscured my eyes.

I heard a far-off yelling. "Steve, stop that! Steve!"

My father laughed as he pulled me back onto the trail. I collapsed into a shivering, blubbering mess. My mother knelt and hugged me tightly. I clamped my arms around her as I bawled big, hiccupping sobs into her shoulder.

"What a horrible thing to do!" she shrieked at my dad. "How could you do that to your own child? Don't you ever do that again!"

Dad bent down and looked at me. "You don't push anyone while hiking. Barry could have fallen all the way down to the rocks." He stood and looked at Mom. "And don't worry, I wouldn't have let go."

Slowly, the fear and trembling subsided, but I couldn't stop crying.

"Let's get going." I heard the impatience in my dad's voice.

Then my stomach heaved, and I was sick all over Mom's blouse.

"Aw, that's disgusting," Barry hollered.

Mom eventually released me, and I stood. Barry snickered and pointed. I looked down and felt my face go red. Not only had I been sick, I'd also peed my pants. After some arguing, my parents decided to head to our campsite and then home. Barry and Dad were irritated and hurried ahead. I don't remember much about the hike back down except that I stayed on the inside of the trail until Mom and I were on flatter ground. I huddled in the back seat on our return trip home. It was a long time before I was able to sleep a whole night without having a nightmare about falling from somewhere. And I became afraid to go anywhere that had a view, like the second story of a mall or a room with a balcony.

Apparently, my father thought the whole thing a joke because from then on, he teased me about my fears, and if someone was around at the time, he'd tell the story of when I'd wet my pants. Of course, he'd gloss over the fact that he had held me over the edge of a cliff.

As I grew up, I became morbidly fascinated with the thought of falling. I began to imagine how long it would have taken me to hit the ground. What part of me would have landed first? If I had fallen facedown, would I have seen the rocks coming at me? If I'd fallen backwards, would I have felt the landing? And, most of all, I wondered what my thoughts at the end would have been.

I listened to my friends talk about their ziplining experiences and watched people cliff dive, hang glide, or bungee jump on television. Just seeing them step out over nothing knotted my stomach and sent waves of dread through my brain. And yet I listened and watched, mesmerized.

My fascination transformed from me plummeting through the air to other people plummeting through the air. I read stories about people who had fallen to their deaths from buildings, bridges, and cliffs. I looked for any comment that would answer my questions about which way they had landed and how long it had taken them to hit the ground.

I also began to speculate what their thoughts would have been while they were in the air between the solid base they left and the landing they made. What were they thinking in the last seconds of their lives? Was it about family, friends, things they hadn't done, places they hadn't seen? Were they so consumed by fear that they had no thoughts? If they were committing suicide, did they realize their mistake and change their minds at the last moment when it was too late?

I decided I would never know.

But, one Saturday evening during my first semester at college, I was given the opportunity to find out how long it took to fall. I had been invited to a birthday party by the friend of a friend. I arrived to find that the address was an apartment building, and the apartment was on the 12th floor. I stood in the foyer and stared at the flashing numbers as the elevator worked its way down to the ground floor. The doors opened. People got off and others on, and the doors closed. As the numbers went up and then down again, I had a mental argument, trying to convince myself that it would be okay. This was my first party invitation of any type, and I wanted to be part of it. I decided I would only hang out in the living room.

There was no one else in the foyer when the doors opened again. I almost changed my mind and walked away but forced myself to enter. On the 12th floor I felt safe walking along the corridor because there were no windows to look out. When I entered the apartment, the crowded living room/kitchen combination throbbed with music. Male and female students talked, laughed, kissed, and generally milled around. Many were already drunk or high, and the air was hazy with cigarette and marijuana smoke. Someone slapped a can of beer into my hand. I saw where the patio doors opened onto the balcony. I went over to the wall opposite them and leaned against it.

I am not a smoker of any kind, so it wasn't long before the smell began to give me a headache. It was either leave the party or go stand at the patio doors for some fresh air. Again, it took some convincing before I went to hover by the door frame. Students were constantly going in and out. Many were smoking. I sighed. It was time to go back to my dorm room.

Then I saw a guy hanging over the railing, being sick. I stood, riveted. He was leaning out over empty space, just as I had years earlier, only he was doing it of his own free will. Didn't he know he could fall? Maybe he was too drunk to understand.

I stepped outside. My heart raced and sweat broke out on my upper lip and under my arms. I felt a liquid on my hand and looked down to see that I had crumpled the beer can. I dropped the can, took a deep breath, and slowly let it out. I wondered how long it would take him to hit the ground if he fell. I wondered whether he would land faceup or down. I wondered what his last thoughts would be. I wondered if I could really do it. My desire to know fought with my fear of heights, and it eventually won.

Someone yelled, “Happy Birthday!” in the living room. The students filed through the door, leaving just the sick guy and me. I sidled over, not going near the railing. That would have been expecting too much of me. I stretched my hand out, then pulled it back without touching him. I could hear ‘Happy Birthday’ being sung. Again, I looked around. We were still the only ones on the balcony. I glanced at my watch, then bent and grabbed his legs and lifted. He disappeared over the edge with just a startled yelp.

I wanted to relish my success but knew I had to protect myself. I stepped back into the living room. Cake was being passed around. A group was at the door leaving, so I joined them. Some of them staggered down the hallway, helped by friends not much more sober. I grabbed an arm. As we waited for the elevator, the apartment door flung open, and partiers emerged in a chaotic and tangled mess. I held my breath, waiting for one of them to accuse me of being a murderer. They looked down the hall and saw us at the elevator. They must have decided the stairs would be faster because they ran in that direction. The elevator came, and we entered and rode it down to the ground floor. I’m not sure they were even aware I was with them.

We parted once we were outside, and I hurried away from the building.

The next morning, stories about the student who had been so drunk he had fallen off the balcony during a party spread quickly through the dorms. It was also speculated that he had jumped after breaking up with his girlfriend. Pictures of him lying on the grass, his arms and legs askew, blood and brains everywhere, were circulated by everyone who had rushed down to check on him. Those pictures showed that he had landed on his back.

Apparently, the police had taken the names of the partiers, then sent everyone home. As I walked to my first class, I saw police cars parked on the streets and officers speaking to my fellow students. I listened to the conversations afterwards, and it seemed that no one had seen him topple over. They’d all been singing ‘Happy Birthday’. Since no one remembered I had been there, the police didn’t talk to me. I tried to maintain my composure, to act normal the next week, to hide my elation at what I had done and to quell my anxiety at being found out. When it was eventually ruled an accident, I was finally able to relax. The incident was soon forgotten by everyone but me.

I reveled in what I had done. I reveled in what I had learned. It took him just over four seconds to hit the ground. That's how long I had stood on the balcony, sweat running down my back, until the thump. It was faint and hard to hear over the noise in the living room, but I'm sure I heard it. So, two of my three questions were answered that night. And I was satisfied for a few years.

I graduated, found a job, and began dating. Nothing serious, just enough to make it look like my life was normal. But people plunging from heights became an obsession.

I hadn't thought about climbing the tower when I turned off the highway. I just wanted to see the view from the deck at its base. I stood back from the railing and took some pictures with my cell phone.

"Why don't you want to?" the young woman asked the young man.

He leaned his arms on his knees and looked down at his hands. "Because I'm afraid of heights."

"You are?" She sounded surprised.

"Yes. I probably won't make the first set of steps."

"Oh."

I craned my neck and looked up to the top of the tower. It rose high above the treetops into the blue sky. As I listened to the young couple's discussion, I wondered if I could climb up there.

"But you go," the young man encouraged. "I'll have a nap in the car."

I checked for cameras. When I first started my pursuit for enlightenment, few places had installed them, but they are becoming more and more popular and now limited my activities. I left the couple to decide what they were going to do and walked up the stone steps to the first flight of metal stairs. These steps were easy for me to climb because they were still close to the ground. I hesitated on the second landing. The metal railing came up to my waist, and through it, I saw the couple kissing below.

The next time the mania took over was when I was in San Francisco for a week making a presentation for the company I worked for. The Golden Gate Bridge is known as the 'death bridge' or 'suicide bridge' because it is one of the most frequently used places in the world for people to commit suicide. Since its opening in 1937, over 2000 people have jumped to their deaths. I went to see this attraction one evening.

Anxiety and dread filled my stomach as I started across it. I waited for the panic to well up in my chest and take over my mind as it had at times when I was facing my fear of heights. But it didn't. I stopped walking. My fear was still inside me, but I found myself embracing it. I was excited by it. My mission was helping me master it. I met a few people going in the opposite direction, and there was some traffic as I continued over the bridge. I never got too close to the edge, and I never looked over it. I had conquered part of my phobia but not all of it.

I turned and headed back, and that is when the opening occurred. It was such an opportune time. Just him and me on the bridge, no other walkers or cyclists or vehicles. He even smiled at me and said, "Hi," as we met.

I waited until he was a few steps away listening to his music on his headphones, then snuck up on him and, using his movement, propelled him to the wall where his shoulders and chest bowed over it. I hefted his legs and let momentum carry him over. He barely had time to say, "What…?"

Two days later, when his body was found, his family and friends went on television to express their shock that he had taken his own life.

"He was the last one we would have suspected," said one friend.

He was just some poor guy on his way home after a late shift at work. Too bad he didn't know that I was out prowling, looking for someone just like him.

***

I felt the sweat on my face and hands. I held on tight to the railing and the posts as I climbed higher up the tower. I heard footsteps on the metal steps below me. I listened. Just one set. I had to hurry.

I went from landing to landing, focusing on my task. Then I reached the circular staircases. These were narrower, more confining, as the tower tapered towards the top. I had gone far enough.

I waited, listening to the person climbing closer. I felt hyped. My palms were clammy, my stomach knotted with anticipation. I licked my lips as I heard her on the landing below me.

After my Golden Gate encounter, I began to seek out unsuspecting individuals, and when given the opportunity, I perfected my technique. I followed people; I went on cruises.

Did you know that almost 200 passengers have gone missing from cruise ships in the last decade? And, because some vanished in international waters where jurisdiction was sketchy, their disappearances were seldom reported to the authorities by the cruise lines. Oh, the families knew they didn't get off the ship at the end port, but because no one saw what actually happened to them— whether it was suicide, an accident, or misadventure— nothing could be done.

I have found there are different types of people who take cruises: those who want to see other countries without the hassle of driving there or flying, those who like to be pampered on their holidays, and those who want to leave their normal life behind and spend their time drinking and partying in a safe environment.

Oh, those poor gullible people, thinking they were safe, that they could drink and dance and act the fool because there were no social restraints of family and work like at home. They were so easily picked up, anticipating that an on-board romance would be fun, would be something to brag about when they got back to their normal lives. They were so easily convinced that a walk on the deck before going to their room was a good idea.

And no one notices me. I don't stand out in a crowd, I blend in. That is the first secret to my success. People, when questioned, are usually unable to remember me, let alone describe me.

The second secret is to pick a person alone, preferably smaller, and distracted by a cell phone or music. Surprise is my third secret. I don't give them any warning.

I started down. She looked startled as I approached, for my running shoes with soft tread didn't make any noise. I smiled and saw her relax.

"Quite the view from up there." I pointed with my right hand.

Her eyes followed my gesture, and that's when I reached out with my left hand and grabbed her neck, bending her upper body over the railing. Both her hands clutched my wrist. I stooped and slipped my right hand behind her knees, pulling them up. I let go of her throat and shook her hands off mine. She grasped at some metal crossbars but missed. I raised her knees higher, and she slid out of my grip. I looked at my watch, timing her fall.

Her screams ended when she hit the ground. Three seconds. I clambered down the steps. I looked for the young man to come running. He didn't. The parking lot was too far away for him to have heard her scream.

I saw her body. Her eyes were blank as she stared at the sky. Elated at what I had done, I raced along the trail. At the parking lot, I slowed then walked casually to my vehicle. I drove past the young couple's car and saw that he had fallen asleep on the passenger's side. I smiled as I left the lot.

I'm not like other killers. I don't need to see the person die or listen to them pleading for their life before killing them. I don't need them begging in order to feel powerful. No, I just like knowing that I can do it with no mess, no noise, no weapon to bring along, no body to dispose of, nothing to leave behind as possible evidence against me. All I need is me and the solid feel of my hands on the person. It usually only takes a gentle shove to make them lose their balance and topple over the edge.

Like the woman who was sitting on a fence above a raging river because she wanted to get the perfect picture of the rapids. When she decided to get off the fence, she lost her balance, fell into the water, and was swept away. One little nudge was all it took.

Over the years I have maintained a loving relationship with my family. Barry is married and has three children. He and his family, my parents, and I often gather for birthdays and holidays and sometimes take vacations together.

Even though my mother quit hiking in the mountains after the incident when I was eight, my father continues to go two or three times each summer. I am never asked if I want to join him, but the last time we were together, he did tell me the days he planned on going this summer.

Today is one of the Sundays he mentioned, and I decide to join him as a surprise, show him that I have overcome some of my fear.

I am a little late, so I park beside his car, tie up my new hiking boots, and head along the path after him. I enjoy the walk through the trees and meadows, but then the trail begins to climb up the mountainside. Sweat breaks out on my forehead at the memory of that day when I was eight. My heart thumps, and my stomach tightens when I come to a section with a drop-off to my left. I hesitate, but I promised myself that I would do this. I hug the wall to my right and continue.

Eventually, I see my dad walking ahead of me. I smile when I notice that he has the earbuds in his ears from the iPod I gave him for Christmas. We had spent a lot of time Christmas afternoon downloading his favorite music onto it. I increase my pace until I am behind him.

"Dad," I call.

He doesn't hear me over the music. It's funny how some people are so trusting. I extend my hand and touch his left shoulder so that if he is startled and jumps sideways, he will be on the inside of the trail. I don't want him to fall accidently.

Dad does start a bit. He turns to see who wants to pass him. I enjoy the look of surprise when he sees me. He starts to smile, but I don't give him time to speak. I just want him to see it is me, so he will immediately know why I reach out to give him a shove.

But he steps to the side, away from my hand. Was it inadvertent? He pulls the earbuds from his ears. I don't hear any music. I am puzzled. After all the hours we spent loading the songs, why isn't he listening to them?

"At first I didn't believe it," Dad says.

I cock my head to the side. What is he talking about?

"I thought they were just a twist of fate, but the more I looked into them, the more I realized they weren't."

I have lost the element of surprise; maybe I can still overpower him. But he seems wary and has stepped just out of my arm's length.

"I became suspicious after the person went missing on the last cruise you took. It seemed odd that lightning would strike twice, that someone would disappear from two cruise ships you happened to be on. Then I remembered the student when you were in college. I began going through old news. I read about the woman who had fallen into a river at the very same campground you were staying at, and the young man who had just got a promotion at work and committed suicide while you were in San Francisco."

"Those are just coincidences." I dismiss them with a wave of my hand.

"Then the woman fell from the tower."

"Her death was ruled an accident." I like to keep track of what is decided by the police.

"It was, and I almost believed it, until I found your cell phone the last time you visited. I went through your pictures and found the ones of the tower and the date they were taken."

I am shocked that he would go through my phone and disappointed that he would consider me capable of such heinous crimes. Aren't parents supposed to think the best of their children, believe in them, not sneak around behind their backs? I guess not in my dad's case. I'll have to lock my phone from now on.

I sigh. There is no use denying what I have been doing. Besides, only one of us is going to come off this trail, so it doesn't matter what he knows.

"I created the monster in you that day when you were eight," Dad says. "I take full responsibility for that."

I don't care if he takes responsibility for the way I turned out. I have to get this over with before someone comes along. He slumps as if overcome by guilt, and that gives me my chance. I thrust out both hands. His head comes up, and he looks me in the eye as he deflects my hands, stepping to one side. He puts his hands on my rib cage and pushes. My forward movement takes me over. I scream in shock as many have in the past.

I don't bother to time my fall. I know I will land facedown, and I do watch the ground coming at me. My final thoughts are that my dad set me up by telling me when he was hiking and by not playing the music on his iPod so he could hear me coming. It's amazing how trusting I was…

A CAPITAL OFFENSE

I WAS VACUUMING the living room the day my husband Byron hung up the phone and announced that his literary agent, Ron Higgins, had found a publisher for his novel.

"I've been telling you it was a great idea, Celia," he said to me. "I just had to find an agent who thought the same way, and he had to find the right publisher. They must think it will sell because they offered me a contract and an advance based on just my query and synopsis."

I was so happy that it had finally happened. I thought that now he could relax and enjoy the writing instead of getting so worked up about all those rejection letters. I hated when he yelled and tore the letters into pieces and threw them around the room.

When the contract came in the mail, Byron read it out to me. According to the contract, he had to send the chapters as he finished each of them to his agent, who would read them. When half the manuscript was finished, Mr. Higgins would send it to the publisher. Byron signed the papers, and I brought out the bottle of wine I had bought for the occasion. We had a drink to the millions of copies Byron was convinced the book was going to sell. I didn't expect it to be that many, but I secretly hoped we could buy our own home or take a vacation with his royalties. He told me to phone our friends to come for a party the following evening to help him celebrate.

I made the phone calls and then worked hard the next day making Byron's favourite appetizers, cleaning the house, and getting ready for the party.

Our friends came, and they all seemed to be having a good time congratulating Byron. Everyone had a drink, and I was circulating with a tray of food when Byron began talking loudly.

"Yes, I did send my idea out to a few publishers before I acquired my agent. He's the one who found the publisher. All those who turned me down will sure feel like idiots when it's a bestseller. I'll have the last laugh then."

"Is it a big publisher from Toronto or New York?"

"No, it's a small press in Vancouver."

"Did you get an advance?"

"Of course. All good writers get advances."

"Was it enough to buy a home in Mexico?"

"No, the advance wasn't as big as any of Stephen King's. But this is just my first book. You can be sure that with the success of this one, larger publishing houses will be bidding to publish my next one."

I couldn't take any more of it. I pulled him aside and whispered that he was starting to sound like a pompous ass. He was aghast that I would say such a thing.

"I am not. I'm just telling the truth. Besides, they're all interested. This is as close as they will ever get to a famous published author."

"You're not famous yet," I told him.

"It's just a matter of time." He turned to the crowd. "I'd like to propose a toast to my new book. When you read it, you'll be impressed with my creativity."

Everyone in the crowd raised their glasses and dutifully toasted him. He then said that he would sign their napkins because when he was as popular as Stephen King, they could tell their friends they knew him when he was a struggling writer, that he had been their neighbour.

I worked part-time in a drug store and had a small home business making children's costumes. I used our spare bedroom as my sewing room. One day, as I had just finished sewing the first of fifteen dresses for a dance group, Byron came home early from work. He walked into my sewing room carrying a box and set it on the bed.

"What are you doing home?" I asked him.

"I went shopping today," he said and left the room.

I looked at the box and then up at Byron as he came in again carrying another box. He set it beside the first one.

"What's in those?" I asked as I wrapped the dress in plastic.

"They're part of my new computer."

I was shocked. "What?"

"I just bought a computer, a desk, a printer, paper, a chair, and a bunch of supplies I need for my writing."

I looked after our finances, and I knew we couldn't afford all these things. "We don't have the money. How are you going to pay for it?"

Byron answered nonchalantly, "The store was giving a $100 discount if you bring in your old computer, so I took in my old laptop. The rest I put on the credit card. The advance from my book will cover some of it."

"But you only got $150.00, and ten percent of that went to your agent," I told him.

"Don't worry," he scoffed. "I'll get more when I finish my manuscript and my agent gets it to the publisher. And with this new computer, that won't take me very long."

The house we rented was basementless and only had the two bedrooms.

"Where are you going to put these?" I asked him.

"In here. So, get your stuff out. I need the room."

I was totally confused. "What?"

"You heard me. I have a book contract now. I am a bona fide writer, and I can't write on an old laptop at the kitchen table anymore. I need a real office."

"But where will I put my sewing machine, my material, my patterns?" I needed the space for my business.

"In the garage, throw them away, whatever. Just get them out of there." Byron left the room, and I stood and looked at my things. I admit I was in shock and didn't know what to do.

When Byron returned with another box, he dropped an even bigger bombshell. "And I quit my job."

"What?" That seemed to be my favourite word in this conversation, as I was having a hard time absorbing everything.

"I have to finish my manuscript." Byron was beginning to sound exasperated. "I can't continue to work and get my writing done, too."

"How are we going to live, make our rent payments?" I asked. "I don't earn enough money with my part-time job."

Byron didn't seem to care. "You'll have to get a second job or start working full time."

"But what about my business? I won't have time for my sewing."

Byron really sounded disgusted as he waved his hand around the room. "This isn't a business. It's hardly a hobby. It's time you started contributing some real money. Now get rid of this stuff, so I can set up my new office." And with that, he took some packets of paper out of one of the boxes and handed the box to me. "This will help you get started. And hurry up. I want to set up my office today."

When Byron left again, I slowly began to gather the patterns and materials on the bed into a pile.

Byron returned with yet another box. He stopped in the doorway, an angry look on his face. "What's taking so long?" he demanded.

I was in tears and could barely answer. "I don't…What will I…?"

Byron dropped the box on the floor. He grabbed my bolts of material from the bed and threw them in the empty box. "I don't have time to wait while you have a hissy fit. Get busy. Everything has to go, except the bed. I'm keeping it so I have some privacy."

I looked at him. "Privacy?"

"Yes. If I want to work into the night, then I can lie down when I'm tired and not be disturbed when you get up to go to work in the morning."

My sewing machine and material ended up in a corner of the garage. I took the dress to my customer down the street and told her I was sorry, but I couldn't make the others as I had promised. I returned the deposits.

A week later I got a second part-time job at a grocery store, and when I got home, I opened the door of the spare room to let Byron know.

Bryon was working on his novel on his new computer. “I’d appreciate it if you didn’t interrupt me when I’m working,” was all he said.

“Sorry, I just thought I would let you know that I won’t be home many evenings to make supper.”

Byron waved his hand and went back to work. I closed the door.

For the first few months I thought everything was going well. Byron would be at the computer when I got up in the morning and working hard when I came home from work. I was just earning enough money to keep ahead of the bills, and I was hoping he would finish his manuscript soon and find another job.

One day, though, I answered the phone, and it was Ron Higgins, Byron’s agent. He wanted to speak with Bryon. I knocked on the bedroom door and opened it. Byron immediately began yelling. “Would you quit interrupting me? Haven’t I told you not to talk to me when I am working? I lose my train of thought.”

I handed him the phone. “Your agent wants to talk with you.”

Byron glared at me and grabbed the phone. He took a deep breath, then said pleasantly, “Hello, Ron.”

He listened, and I could see his face turning red. “Yes, Ron. I know I’m late with some chapters. I’ll get them to you by the end of the week.”

When Byron hung up, he turned to me. “From now on, when you have something to say to me, you write it on a piece of paper and slide it under the door. I won’t have time for interruptions.” He threw the phone at me and slammed the door.

That was the first of many phone calls I answered from Mr. Higgins. Apparently, Byron wasn’t sending in chapters on time, and he wasn’t answering Mr. Higgins’ emails about them. Each time, I would reassure Mr. Higgins that I had given Byron his last message and then dutifully write down the new message on a piece of paper and shove it under Byron's door.

My sister Sylvia lives across the country. Before the contract, we kept in touch through emails and Facebook, but Byron wouldn't let me in his room to use the computer anymore. And I had to cancel my cell phone, so I couldn't text her. With only my paycheque coming in, we just had a landline and Internet service for Byron. Long-distance phone calls cost extra. Sylvia wasn't any better off than me financially and couldn't afford to call me either. One day she did phone and asked if Byron would let us email each other twice a week. I didn't think he would agree, but she insisted on sending him an email to ask.

I was dusting the living room when Byron stomped down the hall, his housecoat flapping behind. I wrinkled my nose at the smell of beer and body odor as he neared.

"I printed this off for you!" he yelled, throwing a crumpled piece of paper at me. I cringed. He never talked to me in a decent voice anymore.

I hadn't liked the changes in my husband while he'd struggled to become a published writer, and I certainly didn't like the person he'd become since getting his book contract. There were many times I wished he'd never gotten that contract and even some when I wished I'd never married him.

"I want you to come into my office now and email your sister back."

In his office there were empty beer cans, plates with leftover food, and full ashtrays everywhere. It smelled as bad as he did. On the floor I saw the many notes I'd pushed under the door. I picked some up and asked if he even read them.

"I don't have time," he said crossly.

Byron gestured to the office chair and told me to sit down. I sat and asked him what he wanted me to say.

"What do you think? Tell her not to send any more emails."

In my agitation, I accidently hit the Caps Lock key and starting to type in capital letters.

"Capital letters means you're shouting, dummy," Byron laughed harshly. Then he sobered. "That's not a bad idea. You're going to type the message in capital letters. That way your sister will definitely get the message not to do it again."

"I don't want to shout at my sister," I said.

"If you don't do it, I will," Byron threatened.

So, I typed Sylvia's message in capital letters, then left his office in tears.

I was tired and hungry and decided to make something quick and easy for supper. As I put the lid on the pot with the macaroni, Byron entered the kitchen and yanked open the refrigerator door. "Is that all the beer?" he asked, peering in.

"I guess so."

"Is it too much to ask that there be beer in the fridge?" He grabbed a can and opened it.

"I bought a dozen yesterday."

"Are you saying I drink too much?"

Byron had claimed other writers like Dashiell Hammett and Raymond Chandler drank while writing, and it made them more productive. From the number of phone calls from his agent about late chapters, I guessed it wasn't working for him.

"What's for dinner?" He lifted the lid from the pot.

"Macaroni and beans," I answered.

"Geez." He slammed down the lid. "Can't you fix anything decent?"

"Hey, I worked all day!"

"Are you insinuating I didn't?"

I sighed and wished, again, that I'd never married him.

The next evening, I put oil on to heat for french fries, then went to have a quick shower. It felt so good I spent more time under the soothing water than I'd intended. When I stepped out of the shower, I could smell smoke. I donned my housecoat and hurried to the kitchen. The oil had caught fire, and it had spread to the cupboards and curtains. The living room and hallway were filling with smoke.

I coughed as I hurried down the hall to warn Byron, then rushed next door to call the fire department. I returned to our yard, but Byron wasn't there. When the trucks arrived, I ran up to the fire fighters.

"My husband's still in there!" I cried.

The firemen tried entering the house but were driven back by the heat and smoke. An hour later the fire was out, and an ambulance had taken Byron's body away.

"I set the oil on the burner and went for a shower," I explained to the police officer who was questioning me. "When I came out, there was smoke everywhere."

"Then what did you do?" she asked.

"I ran next door to call the fire department." I dabbed my eyes.

"Did you warn your husband?"

"Oh, yes. I shouted at him," I said, thinking of the word FIRE I'd printed three times in capital letters on a piece of paper and shoved under his door.

Acknowledgements

Big thank you to the staff at RCN for editing the stories and putting this collection together.

Firebrand
by Mary Walz

Dangerous.

That's how sixteen-year-old Saray sees herself.

As both a magikai in a land where magic is outlawed and an orphan who was abandoned by her parents to boarding school, Saray has been taught to view her abilities as a threat.

When Saray's talents are accidentally revealed, she is forced to flee her school. But she is given hope by a sympathetic teacher in the form of the Isle of Dundere - a place where Saray can find safe haven for her magic, and where her blind friend Trina can seek healing for her vision.

As they make their way, though, Saray and Trina will learn that much of what they've been told is a lie. To reach Dundere, they will need to face their own prejudices and depend on people they've been taught to fear. And Saray will learn things on her journey that will challenge her beliefs about both her own origins and the magic within herself.

Because Saray's magic IS dangerous. But danger can be useful when it's wielded skillfully.

Step into a world full of forbidden magic and found family. Firebrand is an exciting addition to Canadian fantasy. - Christine Lavallée

Available wherever books are sold

RCN Media Store
Chapters
Amazon
Barnes & Noble
or your favorite bookstore

Get your exclusive copy and more at **www.rcn.media/store**

www.ingramcontent.com/pod-product-compliance
Lightning Source LLC
LaVergne TN
LVHW050343160826
845677LV00014B/3763

* 9 7 8 1 9 8 9 8 9 8 9 3 2 *